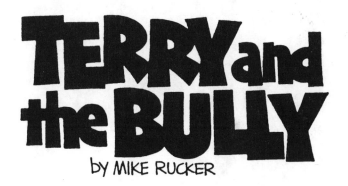

TERRY and the BULLY

by MIKE RUCKER

SECOND EDITION

UNIVERSITY EDITIONS, Inc.
1905 Madison Avenue
Huntington, West Virginia 25704

Cover and interior art by Bob Burchett

"You cannot shake hands with a
clenched fist."   — Indira Gandhi

The Licensed Trademark of the elevated sprocket design illustrated
is owned and registered by Caterpillar Inc. Used by permission.

Dedication

For Heidi

Tractor equipped with a winch

Big trucks rumbled along the highway. They were taking Terry the Tractor and his friends to a new job.

By evening they were all there and they lined up together.

The boss came by and told them, "Okay, everyone get a good night's sleep. We'll get started early tomorrow."

Then he got into his truck and drove away.

"Durn," said Monte Motorgrader, "he didn't tell us what kind of job this is."

"I heard we are going to build a huge dam," answered Suzy Scraper.

"Hot dog!" yelled Terry. "This will be lots of fun."

"You are really dumb, Terry," jeered Thurman Tractor. "I never met anyone so silly as you. I think you really do like to work."

"Leave Terry alone," said Suzy. "Terry always works hard and enjoys what he does. Isn't that what machines are supposed to do?"

That night the machines were so excited they could hardly sleep. Terry wondered if he would ever get any rest at all.

He was nearly asleep when an owl suddenly flew down and landed on Terry's hood.

"Whoo, whoo?" he screeched, so loudly that Terry's eyes snapped open wide.

"Oh, hello Mr. Owl," answered Terry. "You are an owl, aren't you? I've heard that owls say 'Whoo'."

"Of course I'm an owl, that should be obvious! But my question was who are you?"

"I'm Terry and these earthmoving machines are my friends. Tomorrow we are going to start building a big dam."

"What's that funny thing there?" asked Owl, pointing.

"That's my bulldozer," answered Terry. "I use it to push dirt. I can even push down trees with it," he proudly boasted.

But that upset the Owl very much. "You won't push down my tree, will you? My home is in a hollow tree."

"Oh, I don't think so," replied Terry. "Where is your tree? I hope it isn't near the river."

"It's high up on the hill."

"Good, I'm sure it will be safe," said Terry. "In fact, I'll make sure your tree is safe."

"What's that strange looking thing there?" Owl asked pointing to the back of Terry's frame.

"That's my winch. It has a long wire rope. I use it to pull heavy loads."

Just then, the sun popped over the hill.

"Oh, oh!" Owl said. "I've got to hurry back to my tree. I like to be in bed by this time, so I can get a good day's sleep." And away flew Owl to his hollow tree.

Terry thought, "That's strange. I sleep at night, but he sleeps during the day. Mr. Owl is certainly different, but I like him, anyway."

Now the sun was up and the machines were wide awake and their engines were all revved up. They were all excited about the new job!

"Let's go to work," shouted Monte Motorgrader. All the machines scrambled down the hill. Soon each was hard at work.

Terry started to push dirt with his bulldozer. Linda Loader was digging dirt. Monte Motorgrader was trying to make a smooth road.

Even though each machine was working hard, soon they were all causing problems for each other.

Linda dug a hole right where Monte was trying to make a road. "Hey!" he shouted, "Stop that! Can't you see you're messing up my work?"

Linda snapped back, "Why don't you go someplace else?"

Just then Suzy Scraper ran into Timmy Truck. Timmy tried to back up, but Linda was right behind him. Each machine wanted to do its own job and they weren't thinking about anyone else's job. The air was filled with yelling, honking and exhaust fumes.

"Stop!" someone shouted. The machines stopped and looked. It was the boss. "You must work together," he scolded. "Each of you has an important job to do. But to work together you must have a plan. See what a mess you make if you don't have a plan?"

The machines all agreed. All except Thurman, that is.

He mumbled, "I can work just fine without any dumb plan."

The other machines lined up together so the boss could give each machine a job and a place to work.

Terry's place was special. It was on the hill where Owl lived. He was pleased to work there so he could protect Owl's tree.

The sound of Terry's powerful engine awakened Owl.

"What's all the racket out there?" he asked blinking his sleepy eyes.

"It's just me, Mr. Owl. It's your friend Terry."

"You're no friend if you have to make all that noise! All that racket is keeping me awake. I'll bet you're here to try to push down my tree."

"Oh, no!" cried Terry, "I wouldn't do that. In fact, that's why I want to work here. I want to make sure no one hurts your tree."

"Well see that they don't!" snapped Owl. With that, he popped his head back inside.

Terry felt very bad. He wanted to be Owl's friend and protect Owl's home. But Owl didn't seem to want Terry's friendship.

"Maybe I'll just go someplace else to work," thought Terry.

The more he thought about Owl, the madder he got.

Finally, he shouted at Owl, "I'm going away. I don't care if someone does push down your tree." And he started down the mountainside.

Owl flew out of his tree calling to Terry. "I'm sorry, Terry. I was so sleepy I didn't know what I was saying."

Terry stopped when he heard Owl's friendly voice.

"That's okay. I'm sorry, too," he replied.

So they decided to be friends after all. Owl welcomed Terry back to his tree.

Every day after that Terry went back to work near Owl's tree. It was his special work place. He moved lots of dirt there and made the ground smooth. He was very careful not to disturb Owl's tree.

One day when Terry came to work, Thurman Tractor was in his place. He was pushing dirt right where Terry had made the ground nice and smooth. He was messing up everything!

"You're not supposed to be here. Get out of here!" Terry shouted, as he dashed up to Thurman. "This is my place to work. It's part of the plan."

"Aw, who cares about that stupid plan?" laughed Thurman. "I'll work anywhere I want. And you're not big enough to stop me!"

Terry was really mad. He knew Thurman was doing things wrong. And, he wasn't going to let Thurman run him off his special work place.

"You bully!" he screamed at Thurman.

He tried to push him away. But Thurman was just too big. Terry could not push him at all.

Thurman turned and put his bulldozer right against Terry's. Then he began to push. Terry pushed back, but it was no use. Thurman was so much bigger and stronger.

Thurman started pushing Terry down the hill. Terry spun his tracks as fast as he could, but down he went further and further. Thurman pushed Terry a long way down the mountainside.

"Take that, Shrimp!" Thurman said. "If you want more, come on back. I'll give you a real whipping next time."

Then he went back to push dirt around spoiling all the hard work Terry had done.

Big tears came into Terry's eyes. He was really mad now.

"You're not being fair!" he cried.

He scrambled back up the mountain. He ran as fast as he could right at Thurman. Thurman saw him coming. But could not get out of the way.

Terry hit Thurman hard, right in the side. But Thurman was big and tough. He was not hurt.

The boss drove up just in time to see Terry hit Thurman.

He shouted, "Stop that! I won't have fighting on my job."

Terry felt awful. He was afraid he was going to cry. Then he heard Thurman taunting him. "You're gonna get it now, Shrimp!" he snarled.

Terry was angry and ashamed and a little bit hurt, all at the same time. There was only one thing to do: run away!

Down the mountain he dashed as fast as he could go! He heard the boss call out, "Stop, Terry!" But he didn't listen.

He kept running until he reached the other side of the mountain. He went behind some big rocks, hoping no one would ever find him there.

He was so hurt and confused! He had tried to do a good job. He had worked as hard as he could, but now everything was ruined. He decided he would never go back. He would stay there until he turned into a big lump of rust.

Soon it got dark. Bats swooped past him, and animals prowled around. Terry knew they wouldn't hurt him, but he was still a little bit frightened. A bunny hopped past looking for fresh dandelions to nibble. An old raccoon called out, "What are you doing here?" But Terry didn't answer. He would never speak again.

Meanwhile, Terry's friends were out looking for him. Owl had been flying around for hours, searching everywhere. Finally, he saw Terry's hiding place. He swooped down and landed on a nearby rock. Terry was startled until he recognized Owl.

Then, forgetting his resolution never to speak again, Terry said, "Oh, hello."

"Hello, indeed!" replied Owl. "Don't you know everyone has been looking for you all night?"

"Looking for me?" asked Terry. "Why?"

"Why? Because they're your friends. And because they like you and want you back."

"I don't believe it! Just go away and leave me alone."

"Okay," said Owl, "If that's what you want, I'll just go away."

But, he didn't just go away. He flew around until he found the boss. He landed right on the hood of the truck, hopping up and down and pointing toward Terry. At first the boss did not understand. He tried to chase Owl away.

"I have no time to play games," he said. But Owl kept hopping and pointing.

At last the boss understood. "Okay, lead me to Terry."

Away flew Owl, with the boss following close behind.

Terry was still feeling miserable. He was thinking about how unfair Thurman was. His headlight eyes filled with tears. He thought he saw lights coming. But he couldn't be sure because his eyes were so blurry.

"Oh, my!" he thought, "I hope that isn't someone looking for me."

But he didn't really mean it. He hoped Owl was right about his friends liking him and wanting him back.

The boss drove up to Terry and said, "You should be ashamed of yourself! We've all been worried about you."

"About me?" asked Terry. "I'm sorry. I thought you were mad at me."

"Well, I was angry. That was pretty silly of you to hit Thurman like that."

Tears came into Terry's eyes again.

"Okay," the boss said, "that's enough of that. Now, Terry, let me tell you something. I know everything that happened between you and Thurman."

"You do?" asked Terry, his eyes wide in amazement.

"Yes. I know how Thurman messed up your special work place. I also know what a fine job you did there, and how hard you worked. Now come back with me. We have a full day's work ahead of us."

Owl circled overhead crying out, "Yes, Terry, come back. I need you to protect my tree."

So Terry followed the boss back to the job site. They arrived just as the sun came up. The other machines saw Terry coming and ran up to see if he was all right. This made Terry feel much better. He saw that his friends did miss him. He was glad to be back.

Then the boss said, "All right, Terry and Thurman, now apologize to each other."

Neither wanted to, but the boss insisted. Terry finally said in a soft voice, "I'm sorry." But he only half meant it because he was still mad at Thurman.

Thurman said, "Me too, I guess." He didn't mean it at all.

The boss called out, "Okay, let's go! We're behind in our work."

Terry watched the other machines go back to their work places. Then he asked the boss, "Where should I work?"

The boss looked surprised and said, "Why, back at your special place, of course. You did very good work there, just like the plan called for."

That made Terry feel much better. He went back to his work place. He found that Thurman had not messed it up very much after all. As he worked he sang this song:

MUSIC ON PAGE 60

Terry worked hard all day, and felt very good—tired, but good. Then, near the end of the day, he heard hollering on the mountainside below him. He hurried down to see what was wrong.

Someone yelled, "A tractor almost fell over the cliff. He can barely hold on."

"Who is it?" asked Terry.

"It's Thurman. He was showing off by getting too close to the edge," answered Monte Motorgrader.

"It serves him right," said Linda Loader. "He always has been a show off and a bully."

"That's enough of that kind of talk!" someone said. It was the boss, who had just arrived.

They all looked down at Thurman Tractor. He was on a narrow ledge on the side of the cliff. He could not go backwards or forwards without falling off. Thurman really looked scared.

"Hang tight," the boss shouted to Thurman. "I've got a plan."

Then he said, "Terry, come with me. Only you can save Thurman."

"I don't understand," thought Terry. "There's nothing special about me."

"You are the only tractor here with a winch," explained the boss. "You must use it to save Thurman. Just do as I tell you."

First, the boss tied Terry firmly to Owl's tree. Then he pulled the end of the wire rope from the winch down the cliff. He fastened it to Thurman.

"Now," he told Terry, "pull with all your might."

Terry did pull! He pulled so hard he thought his tracks would come off. But Thurman was so big and heavy that he didn't move. Instead, Owl's tree began to shake.

Owl was terribly afraid that his tree would be pulled down. But he was even more worried about something else. If the tree broke, both Terry and Thurman would fall into the river below. They would both be broken into bits.

Terry pulled and pulled and pulled. At last he began to inch Thurman up the cliff. It was such hard work he almost had to quit. He was so tired! But he told himself that he had to save Thurman.

Finally the job was done. Thurman was safe. The boss and the machines crowded around Terry.

"You are a real hero," Suzy Scraper told Terry.

"Oh, no I'm not. I only did what had to be done."

"Well, I'm proud of you, Terry," said the boss.

Thurman came over and said, "Thank you, Terry, for saving me. I'm sorry I was such a bully. I'll never do that again."

Terry said, "I'm sorry I hit you. I'll never do that again. I was just mad. That's all."

The boss said, "Let's have a cheer for both Terry and Thurman." He shouted, "Hip, hip, hooray!"

All the machines revved up their engines and honked their horns. Owl flew around overhead, as proud of Terry as could be, and glad that his tree was safe.

Terry and Thurman stood side-by-side, smiling. And both thought how nice it was not to be enemies.

"Being mad at someone makes me feel so bad," thought Terry, "but being friends is really cool. I guess to have a friend you need to be a friend."

TERRY'S PLANNING SONG

by SHERRY SECKLER

About the Author

Mike Rucker has more than thirty-five years experience with tractors as an employee of Caterpillar Inc.

He originally wrote stories about Terry the Tractor for his son Derek.

Mike indicates that Terry's personality is actually based on that of Derek. "He is the most earnest person I know. He has strong feelings about right and wrong, just like Terry the Tractor."

"I want kids to learn a bit about the working world in my stories. But, just as important, I want them to learn something about themselves—and about life."

Mike dedicates this story to his niece Heidi.

Photo of Heidi at age 3 (1972)

The Illustrator

Bob Burchett has lived in Florence, Kentucky 31 years with his wife Noni on a 13 acre plot they share with their pets. Bob says, "At one time we had 9 dogs. When I went to buy dog tags one time, they gave me a kennel license so we could save money on dog tags. We are now down to only 4 dogs (3 pictured), 5 cats, 2 horses and an iguana."